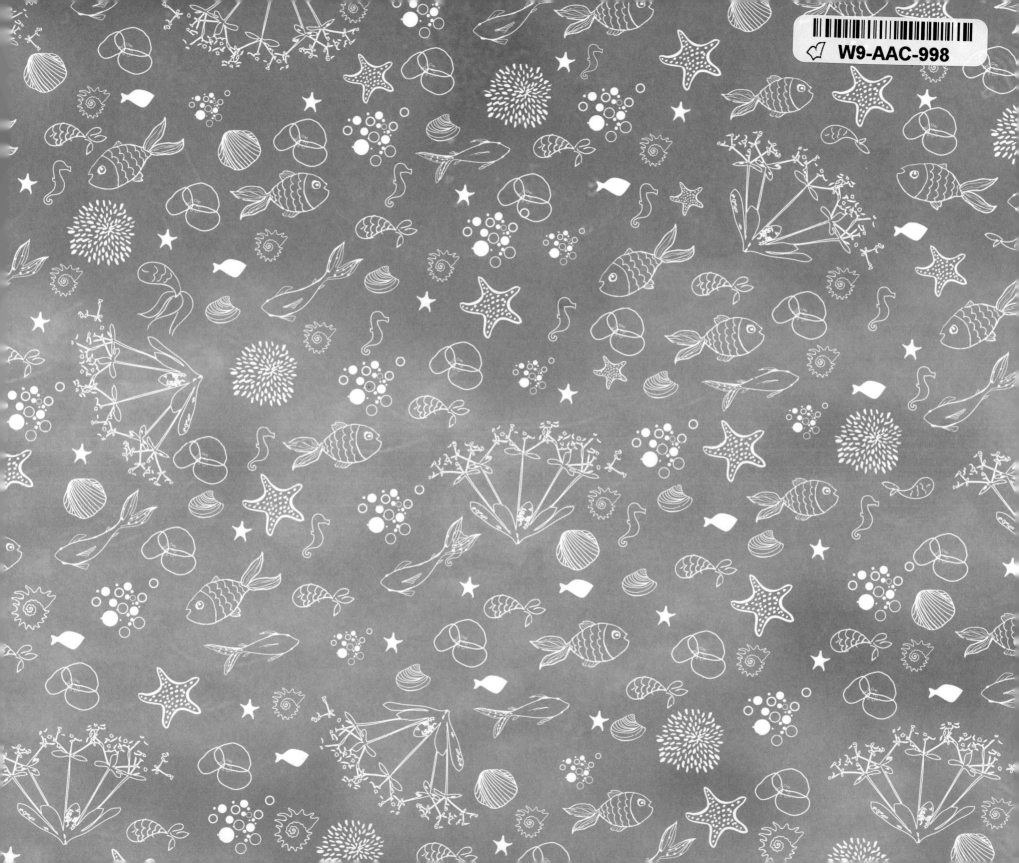

The Ocean Story

written by John Seven

illustrated by Jana Christy

PICTURE WINDOW BOOKS
a division of capstone

The Ocean Story is published by Picture Window Books

a division of Capstone

151 Good Counsel Drive, P.O. Box 669

Mankato, Minnesota 56002

Visit us at www.capstonepub.com

Library of Congress Cataloging-In-Publication data is available at the Library of Congress website.

Summary: The story of the ocean is as old as the earth itself. Overfishing, pollution, and oil spills have

highlighted the need to take better care of our oceans so that the story can continue to be told.

Artistic Effects: Shutterstock/grzhmelek, Lavanda, LittleLion Studio

ISBN: 978-1-4048-6785-7

Printed in the United States of America
in North Mankato, Minnesota.

122010

005970CGS11

For Harry and Hugo
and all our time spent clambering in tidepools, walking beaches,
and spotting whales along the coasts of New England
and at the Bay of Fundy.

Why is the ocean so very big?
It needs to be big to hold a story that is so very old.

Did you know that you are part of the ocean story?

Each time you float in a boat

or hunt for seashells

or hop around in the rain

or sip some water,

you are in it.

The whole world is drenched in the ocean story.
Water from the ocean turns into clouds.

Then the water rains back down on the earth. Rain falls on the flowers and the grass and the trees and the food that farmers grow.

It falls on the sidewalks dotted with slugs, and the highways covered in puddles. And it falls on you, too.

The ocean story is a splendid circle. Everyone everywhere is part of it.

The ocean story is the story of many years and

scores of creatures who have homes

beneath the waves.

Some swim high and pop through to the surface.

Others lurk in the deep dark down below.

So many creatures are part
of the ocean story.

The biggest are blue whales.
They are beautiful singers.
There aren't many left, so listen to the songs carefully.

eeeeeee

click click

Squeak

The smartest creatures are their cousins, dolphins.
They are almost as clever as you.
Their words are whistles and clicks.

Some of the ocean creatures are beautiful but dangerous, like jellyfish.

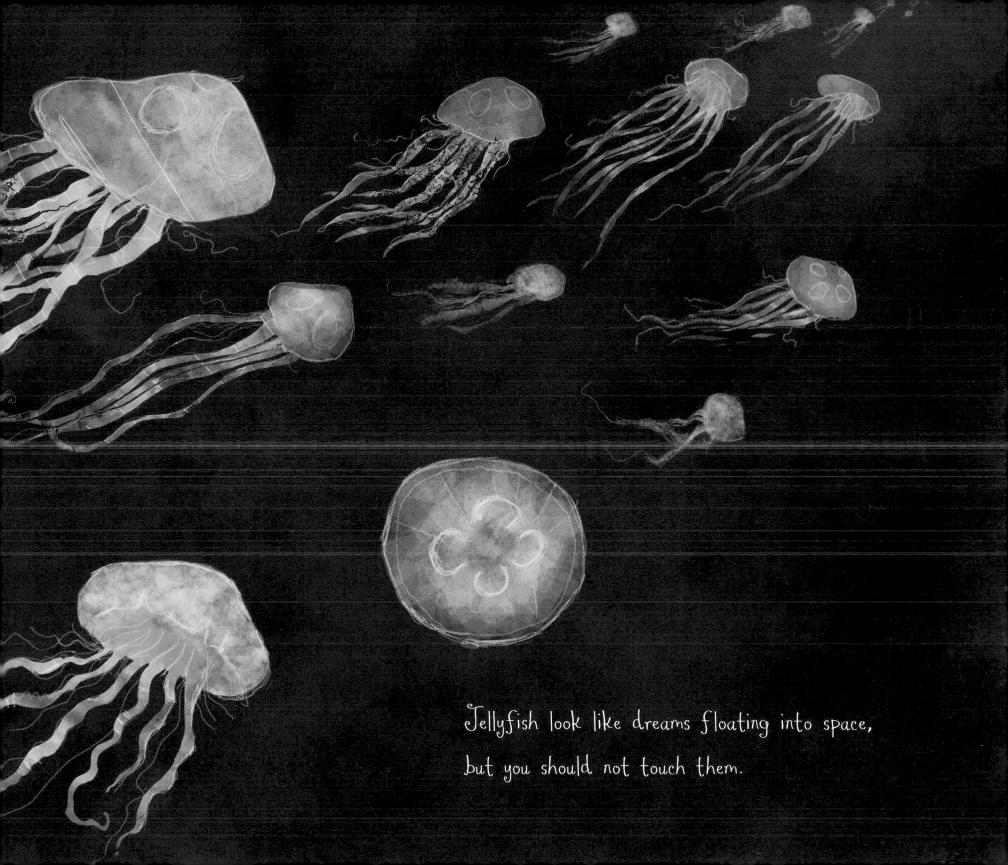

Jellyfish look like dreams floating into space,
but you should not touch them.

There are many strange creatures. You could never decide which one is the strangest. They are all mysterious and unique, hidden below the surface.

Deep Sea Cucumbers

Hammerhead Shark

Flamboyant Cuttlefish

Crinoids

Nudibranches

Juvenile Smooth Trunkfish

Tunicates

Blobfish

Sun Sea Star

Axolotl

Serpent Sea Star

Sometimes the ocean story is filled with wind and waves and fury.

Sometimes the water is covered in sludge and goo and trash and other messy things. Things that should not be in the ocean.

Even deeper down than the deepest creatures,
oil is hidden in the ground under the water.

Oil runs our cars and warms our homes.
We try to pull it out with care.

But sometimes, things go wrong.
Oil goes where it should not be.

The strange, mysterious, and wonderful ocean creatures watch the ocean turn very dark all around them.

The darkness spreads through the ocean.
It wraps around the ocean creatures. Nothing can live in oil.

Sometimes, the ocean story is a scary one.

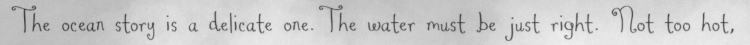

The ocean story is a delicate one. The water must be just right. Not too hot,

not too high,

not too low,

not too empty,

not too dirty.

The ocean story and the earth story are part of each other.
They must be told together. If we all do our part, we can
tell the ocean story again and again and again, forever.